CW00501602

For Wendy
with Love
from David and Judith.
June 2008

Into every life a little Rainbow should fall.
No Rainbow; no Dingley Press.

Frontispiece

Ah, Shadows!
Is it you who recognise me?

For
Jinx & Futura;
my
Polestars

The Creatures In the Night

Written and painted
by
CLIVE WILKINS

DINGLEY PRESS

A DINGLEY PRESS
LIMITED EDITION
© Copyright 2008

CLIVE WILKINS

A CIP catalogue record for this title is
available from the British Library

ISBN-13 978-0-9547083-3-7

DINGLEY PRESS
16, Church Lane, Dingley LE16 8PG UK

Illustrations

1. *And So to Bed*

[Clara goes to bed]

Night follows the day
Each time in a new way
The realities of the day are absorbed
By the fantasy of NIGHT!

The solidness of day
slides
into
the formlessness of a dreaming realm.

See now, Night's cloak drape.
See the folds & the imaginings it
creates & implies.
Folds smooth, folds sublime.
Folds creased, twisted & only seemingly confused.
Folds to suit your personality
Or,
simply, your destiny.

And so to bed!

Night follows the day.

Here we are, 'voyeuragers' at our own story
seen through
the eyes of Clara-
a girl, simple, sweet & tired.

◯

2. *The Fall Into Sleep*

[Clara falls asleep and begins to dream]

A nest, a box, a bed
A room, a womb, a tomb.
A 'top' within which to spin thoughts.
See, fancy free, the ideas are whirling within.
These same thoughts which,
Forced to stand their ground during this day,
Now escape &, pushing 'pell-mell'
Bubble, rush free, surface & float
Off to the realms of fantasy
Where spirits collect their essence & splendour.

All this,
Revealed to us
Under the light of the Moon,
By the guardian spirits of all our thoughts & ideas.
Beings of our own making;
they know that we could not exist without them.

Which came first?
The chicken or the egg?
The dream or the dreamer?

☽

3. The Waking of Dreamfaerie

[Clara must first awaken the Dreamfaerie. He looks after her whilst she dreams]

Asleep & now dreaming
Ready for this night's great adventure.

Clara must first awaken her guardian.
He is Dreamfaerie.
For him.
The day
is a time for sleep
& Night,
when woken by Clara,
brings his true vocation into being.

He,
The purveyor of dreams,
The bringer of truths.
The explorer of worldly knowledge, the clearer of mists,
The teller of myths,
The magician at our nearest gate!

◑

4. The Six Locks

[This is what Clara imagines when she wakes the Dreamfaerie]

Awaken…

Dreamfaerie!

Are there secret keys to open your eyes?

[Looks are like keyes.
Locks are like eyes].

Let the lock open - make your eyes bright.

I see the lock,

I turn the key once to see…
Twice to complete the circle around the eyes,
Thrice to push the key into the dark deep hole in the centre.
Fourth for the watery Blink,
A Fifth secures acceptance of the lock to my will.

It begins to open.

& Sixth.

HE Wakens…

Dear bright mysterious flame

See me! I am Clara!

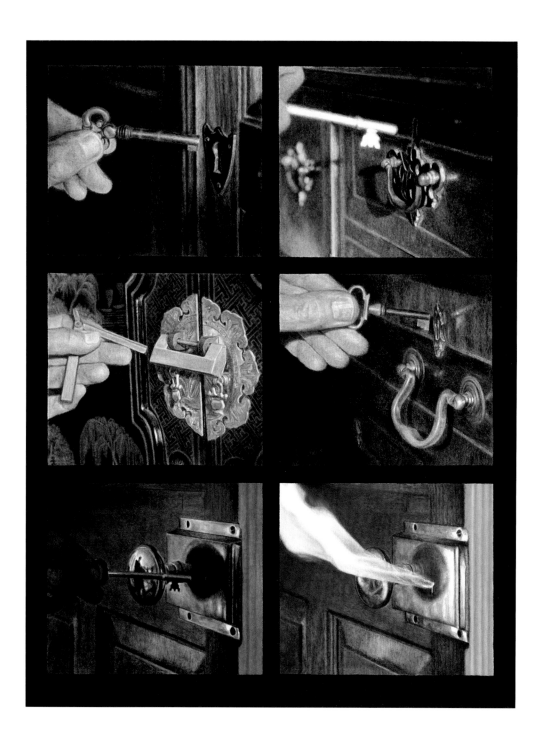

5. The Tray of Dreams

[Dreamfaerie shows Clara a tray of objects from which she may choose her dreams for this Night's adventures]

Dreamfaerie awakes.
The enchantment begins.
The tray of 'What do you require' is brought.

'Here are your questions, Dear Hart,
Meet your dream objects; make your choices.
Which do you explore first?
You have summoned them all—
here within these moments.
In this space, between the near and far gates.
But...
Go no further than that.
If you are to see your daylight world again
you must avoid the space beyond the garden;
beyond that boundary is not for the living.
You see on this tray all that is safe & nice for you.
Ask only these questions
& you will surface,
refreshed & delighted
into your empire & breathing space.
Dear child, let your guide be
SemaPhora;
An exquisite sprite
& friend to the greenest of men.
Turn to see her now!'

A rush of wind & behold! There she is,
amidst the splendour of her art
&
intercepted messages.

●

6. The Meeting of SemaPhora

[Dreamfaerie, being too old to take Clara to her dream creatures himself, uses the help of his friendly servant, SemaPhora, who uses complex words & strange sentences]

Proud, strange SemaPhora speaks without moving her lips. Watch!
Poor Clara cannot understand what she says at all,
Or to what she refers.

◗

'Come child, let the legends & stories of times all be ours.
I am SemaPhora, the angle of principle & fulcrum to all communication
which is subtext & secret.
Know me & understand what I say; & then the language of Nature,
perception & the true meaning of mankind's innermost thoughts
become apparent.
I, listener that I am, hear everything.
I only recognise those things that are not said.
Those things that are not said are the true meaning of all;
the answer is in the spaces, the cracks & the winds of change…
I can see dear Clara that my noble & absurd words are completely lost on you.
…This is maybe all just too clever for YOU!
You are ONLY a child!
Ho-hum! Oh well! If I am to be your guide, let my pride & lofty,
clever words take a fall.
Come child take this simple kiss, proof that I can be a true friend,
I, like a cloak am here to protect you.
We, together, are to fly.
Off to the edge of time & back in through a new window.
We follow the lighthouse beam for safety.
Come waste no time, for now there is none.'

SemaPhora's Texts
'Outside it Snows; so very fast, it is exhilarating to think of it. But please let me continue to lie here,
safe & milky as I am. So warm & secret, so wary of reality'. [German]
'I know I have missed the beginning, what with arriving so late etc. For this I do apologise. However
this is still the first performance is it not? I know I must seem naïve,
but does it not seem to be going on forever? [French]

13

7. The Lighthouse Keeper

[On their journey to this Night's special dream, SemaPhora & Clara stop briefly to meet the Lighthouse Keeper]

'My light is like a star,' he says,
'It's under the stars but, for all that, it's here to be seen.
This light is navigational to dreamers-
Like yourselves indeed.

Well met, you Lovelies!
I see so few spirits these days.
Dreamers, like angels, are in short supply;
Luckily, I enjoy solitude,
thinking and wandering the rocky shoreline.
Best of all, it's the falling stars I watch;
I notice every little change.

So, you'll be travellers this night. The one to guide the other.
My advice is
When you get to the dreamside of the line
Seek the shadows.
Therein lie the secrets.

Avoid the people who cover their faces, or wear masks.
Keep within the house, but, if travelling without,
Stay within the known garden;
That way you will be safe.
Later,
You can, in a flash, return to your daylight world
Using this route.
Good luck, Lovelies!
Bon voyage!'

8. *Masquerade Creatures*

[Clara and SemaPhora arrive back at the same house, strangely different now because it has become a dream. The first creatures that they meet, quite unlike any beings Clara has met before, are having a 'masked' party]

'We are here for the party tonight.
We love your frock.
You are so lovely!
Aren't we too?
Say yes, say yes,yes, say yes,yes,yes!
We are oblivious of all emotions that might hurt.
We love Lord Goodtime.
Stay with us & do nothing
We shall all pretend to be so...HAPPY!'

SemaPhora holds Clara's hand more tightly now.
She is remembering the Light Housekeeper's stern warning.
They turn away,
moving out of the light, into another room of the house.
Here they first notice brighter objects suspended
&
as their eyes become accustomed to the dark...

☽

9. The Magicians in the Shadows

[Here are the secret dreamers who lead the way to where Clara finds friends]

'You have done well to notice us;
We are quiet and here only to watch.
We are shadows.
Do you recognise us?

Not sad, for why should we be?
But happy to delight in the beauty that we see.
All of everything.
Everything to us is poignant, mysterious
&
a delight.

We love all & are happy
to be,
for
as long as is.

We say love, say love love, say love love love!

Dear Clara, you are like us
&
We have gifts for you;
Next door you will find the first of them.'

10. The First Gift - Passing through Walls

[The young Indian boy and his sister Princess Durga are waiting to see Clara]

'It's a push, I'm walking straight through the wall.
LOOK! AT ME!'
says the Indian boy.

'Here's a special gift for Clara;
well illustrated as you can see.
This thing passing through the wall is ME.
It is a curious gift that can be used for
lofty purposes – so I have been told!
Maybe I am too young to know what loftier purposes there are…'
He says, laughing.

The little Princess speaks next.

'You make a joke of everything brother. Be serious, *Darling* Apu!
Let me explain to this dreaming girl.
This boy, he meets no barriers.
He is able,
using skills supreme,
to pass invisibly through this world, it would seem -
meeting no bars or restrictions at all.
[The source of his secret is intent & careful planning]'
Apu & the little Princess speak as one.

'This is yours.'

11. The Second Gift - The Jack in the Box

[Next, the Oriental Chinese Lady presents Clara with a Jack in the Box]

This Oriental lady speaks to Clara in her own language.
She laughs and giggles - *a lot*.

Although she looks so strange,
she moves with
an incredible hypnotic beauty.

Watch!
She is the most beautiful person Clara has ever met!

The Jack in the Box translates everything she says.
He explains that he is a gift from the Chinese lady
& that he belongs to Clara now.

His special tasks are to:
1. Remember the patterns of the stars from both sides.
2. Memorise every known design of snowflake.

...because of this, he says, he will be 'very useful'
when Clara least expects.

12. *The Third Gift - The Seeing of Futures*

[Clara finally meets the Silver Man who has the last of her special gifts; the ability to see different futures that may be possible]

'I've been waiting for you.
I wrote your real name above my fireplace in lipstick,
Long before you were born.
At last, you're here
&
Welcome!
I pass to you the gift of the
M ○ ◐ ◑ ● ◐ ○ N
The seeing of all Futura's using Imagination

IMAGINATION
is all.
And since you have no choice you will,
By necessity,
Move into the future
This is priceless!

With this gift, you can avoid the routes that lead to
DESPAIR.'

'What *are* those routes that lead to despair?'
asks ☾lara.

'Hmm...

See the next room, my dear.'

→

13. The Bandaged Lady

[Clara meets an unhappy bandaged lady whose eyes are brimming with tears]

'I no longer know who I am
or
What I look like'.
says the bandaged lady,
pointing to the door.

'Look, Semaphora,'
says Clara,
'This bandaged lady is so sad and lonely.
I cannot bear to stay here.'

'Nor I, gentle girl.'
whispers SemaPhora,
soothingly.

→

14. The Alienated Man

[Clara & SemaPhora now meet an unhappy Alienated man. He feels he is a stranger in the world]

'Oh! No, NO!

Not in here; move away my pretties.

I am the despair
                                of a frightened MAN
Who owns everything
                                but knows nothing.'

[SemaPhora whispers to Clara]
'His story is strange.
They say he lost faith in himself.
He became the objects with which he surrounded himself
&
became the Thing others expected him to be.

Because he was only trained to perform in the
HUMANCIRKUS,
he forgot what it was he *really* needed to know.

Don't ask me any questions now;'
says SemaPhora,
'I don't really understand any of this either'

'Having now forgotten how to cry.
I am beyond redemption,'
the man sobs.

☺

15. Night Fright

[Clara, glimping the sadness of the last creature, is disturbed & makes herself wake up]

This is just too much for poor Clara.
Fearful & frightened,
She pulls her hand from SemaPhora's grasp
& in the blink of a sleeping eye, awakens.

The Night immediately surrounds the moment.
The Moon, through the window, calms.

A gentle breeze fans.

As the moment fades...

Sleep

&

back

back

↓

16. The Spanish Moon Lady

[On falling back to sleep, Clara meets a very familiar friend, looking more real than ever before]

.......& back

back

&

↓

Ah!

'A speedy return & so soon,'
says the Spanish Moon Lady.

'So lovely...
I am here to protect.
I love.
Be safe with me.

Together, we will gaze at the watery Moon,
through your window & into the sky.'

'I have a dolly like you,' says Clara.

'Nonsense, my child! You are dreaming.'

[The Spanish Moon Lady soon fades into the night & attracted by a strange sound of laughter from the next room, Clara passes through the wall.]

17. The Ambassadors,
Messrs Punch & Moustache

[Clara encounters Mr Punchinello & Mr Moustachio,
her friendly Dream-uncles]

'Yes, plenty of room,'
say the Ambassadors,
'Oh, Yes!
Indeed, we are the Ambassadors, my Dear,
Not always,
But always on this date.
It has always been this way
We're a kind of joke, you know?
We're very funny.'
[Mr Punchinello's leg hurts]
'We are waiting here, quietly,
Peaceful custodians of stored knowledge
& antiquarians
For all the ages that have passed.
We have no new ideas of course;
Only preserving all that has gone on before.
Useful? Oh, Yes!
& friendly uncles, always.
We have our own magic.
It's
a very little magic.'

[Clara will remember them both when she first wakes. They are her Daylight Guardians
whilst the Dreamfaerie sleeps.
They will be with her when she first awakes - hiding where they can be hardly seen.
Only you might discover them, if you search for them-
in the Morning Light.]

18. Girl with Turban

[Continuing on her Night's journey Clara next meets the mirrored girl, who quietly hums a silent tune to herself whilst speaking]

'I am a reflection of what I see,' says the girl in the strange turban,
whilst holding a mirror.
'Is there therefore two of me or only a half?
I can only ever think about myself.
Everything I think is about me.

◐ ◑

I ask myself three questions that I answer with questions –
and supplementary parts!
[Each new question arrives- maybe out of disappointment
with all previous answers]

Question 1. Is this bird which is not in a cage, still in a cage?
Answer. Maybe Yes?
Question 1a. Where can it fly to where the cage will not exist?
Answer.   To places never thought of?
Question 1b. Could the bird exist without the cage?
Answer. I am not sure!
Question 2. Where do these nonsensical words I use come from?
Answer. I have no answer!
Question 2a. How do the ideas in the world fly to me?
Answer. Using these strange puzzles that insist on building themselves
in my poor brain?
Question 3. Does this bird that I love too much, love me?
Answer. I pretend it does…but maybe not?
Question 3a. Why do I ask this?
Answer. Because I want something else to love me as much as I love myself?'

19. War

[Clara, without thinking, wanders into this chaos, but soon decides to take the quickest route into the next room]

'Who am I?

An uncontrolled riot of energy & passion
Is the true beginning of who I am.

I am a thought without a brain;
the most primordial & evil of masks.

The most unkind & demon Diablo
Whose cruelty kills.

I reveal the true animal
On whose foundation
even the most articulate of good people
are built.

Without me, peace would never be so glorious.
Fallen heroes & warriors, never so exalted.

WAR! Here.

Walk around me.

GO...
or stay & be cut!'

20. Sun and Moon Characters

[There's a little play going on here]

These silly & soppy pantomime characters
are here to represent Mama Solar & Papa Luna.
We recognise them so well.

Our beautiful 'gold glow' of Day & our handsome 'white light' of Night.
Neither will interfere with the other's domain.
Parted for all eternity.

Shift workers -
Forever chasing the other with a universal lust
&
Never quite catching that beautiful tantalising tail they chase.

They are the checkerboard of Nights & Days.
The perfect innocent parents.

Ah! the ongoing struggles of move/not move.

The constant ebb & flow of hapless tides.

The incessant cycle of 'we-e' children, coming & going.

The perfect impartial rarefied love of an uncaring Universe.

21. The Siamese Twin

[In this new room Clara meets a most special creature who is made & conceived in equal parts of Art & Nature]

' We are so pleased that you came;
We were wondering which way to go.

Can you show us the way?
Can you explain our dilemma?

Oh! We have so little rest you know?
So much music to write for the Universe.

To aMuse ourselves [Ha Ha!]
We explain ourselves to each other.

One of us is Nature & the other is Art.
Can you tell us apart?
It's easy!

Someone once said,
"Art enhances the defects of Nature.
Art is a beautiful lie."

Can you unRavel that one?
[Hee Hee!]

Naturally, I cannot live without Art.
Nor I without you, dear sister.'

[But Clara wanders off into a corridor, distracted momentarily by a new sound; the sound of a voice calling out.]

22. The Lace-maker

[From an upstairs dressing room, a voice is calling out to Clara]

'Dear dreaming girl,
Yoo-hoo!

Come & sit, do.

My knots & garments are the finest.
They reveal more than they hide.
Delicate work for poor eyes,
but come,
take Tea.

We can talk together in whispers,
giggle & laugh.

I can *even* show you your grown self.

Pass through this small door,
into my dressing room,
past all my worldly garments,
to the Mirror.

See your reflected image,
A vision of Futures to come.'

●

23. Clara in the Mirror

[Clara sees her grown-up self; she looks very lovely]

'But she is
so much like me-
Only older.

I still see the child
in spite of
the lines.

This is perhaps
a mother
of
someone like me.'

[Clara feels rather tearful.
She looks for SemaPhora's comfort & support]

'My sprite, be with me!'

[A faint breeze picks up as, from the shadows, SemaPhora re-emerges]

'Good Love,' she murmurs, 'it is now time for the garden.'

24. The Doorway into the Night Garden

[Clara and SemaPhora now continue the journey through the house. They follow a breeze and soon come to an open doorway leading to the garden]

'From here
your guide need be this plucky man,
GreenMan.
He is a friend & good fellow.

I, poor SemaPhora-
,being but a domestic sprite-
dare not venture abroad this night.

Go see!

Follow this man.
Go where he glows.'

25. GreenMan & Clara in the Garden

*[The Greenest of Men with deep dark eyes introduces Clara to the outdoors
& the Star]*

Not so talkative as to make a noise,
this gentle cloaked figure walks.
Clara
follows.

As if to make conversation
Clara merely points
to the one fixed shining star
that is the Light Housekeeper's joy.

✱

The gentle GreenMan finally rumbles from within,
until,
as emerging from some deep cavern,
part of his infrequently used collection of words
begins to tumble from his lips.

'Ah!
Lovely girl.
You see that which is the Morning Star?
You won't be going *there*.
It lies beyond the manicured garden.
And in the rough places yonder.
No mortal gets the chance, without moving to our dreamside.
It's the greatest glory they say;
those that have been
to the shining place.

The Morning Star!
It's the Gateway to all that's beyond.'

26. GreenMan gives Clara an Opportunity

[The green man gives Clara a rocket, which will allow her to approach the Morning Star]

'GreenMan, is there truly no way of visiting
the Morning Star?'

The gentle creature answers,
'I have for you
this simple artifice to grant your wish.
Using this rocket,
You can get a glimpse of what is there & what lies beyond.

It uses the rude mechanics of your simple daylight thinkers.
But… in some measure, it will get a mortal
Nearer to the Star.'

'You can keep this rocket invisibly about you,
It will always be nearby, ready for whenever you need it.
It's yours, for you alone,
See! That is why it looks like you.'

[Instructions are inscribed in hand written Indian ink]

Take a magic flaming taper,
When you want to hurtle nearer.
Quickly light the blue touch paper,
In a flash, you'll see much clearer.

'Using this rocket you can be sure to return
to the daylight world from whence you came.
This however, must be an adventure for another night,' says the green man,
draping his cloak around Clara
for protection.
'For look there! Lo! Now the morning comes…'

27. Dreamfaerie Wakens our Heroine

[Dreamfaerie calls a halt to the Night's adventure as the morning approaches]

The Morning begins to fast approach.
Dreamfaerie, so vigilant
Calls a halt to the night.

In a moment,
Clara is brought towards
'the time for returns'.

'Dear Girl, do come again;
there will be time anon to continue
and time aplenty for your rocket adventure
on future bold nights.

Here!
Take this section of cloth from my hat.
It will become your remembrance of all that has transpired.
By this remnant, know that we shadows are real.

In daylight, the in-between colours will be bright-
for they represent the Day.
At Night, the main colours between those
will take over
as those first ones fade.

Know us all again
when all colours are equally vibrant;
that signal will denote our presence
& proximity.
This space will then be warm enough for you.
Adieu!
Until the next door opens.
Until the next page turns.'

28. Morning Light

[Clara wakes in the morning]

The day calls our sleeper to wake.
The most wonderful of earthly mornings imaginable.

A
Sleeper
no longer.

The day begins.
The Sun is climbing and is Lord to All.

The memory of the Night fades FAST,
like the colours in Clara's hanky.

...

But Today
is so NEW!

29. Clara in the Morning Garden

[Clara begins a new day. She begins her tasks]

This is the Morning Garden.
Clara has too easily forgotten the Night.

'This cloth has a special meaning,' she thinks,
'But what IS it?'

…We see the daylight overwhelm her Night dreaming world
where all was so recently possible.

The world is filling with brightness.

The intense glow of daylight now spreads too much confusion - it dazzles
concentrated thought - sparkles a new kind of bewitchment - alienating the sleeper's
sensibilities.
The warm milky Clara creature who so recently was intent on finding a home or
nest in a wild dark universe is alive now to only this immediate,
waking, glowing moment.

☼

On the crest of a small breeze, a voice is carried to her ears;

Life's 'washerwoman' under the canopy of Earth's sky is
Calling Clara,

'Darling LOVELY GIRL!'

In a dash & mad frenzy of lively energy,
Our Clara turns away
&,
giggling sheer delight as she runs,
breathing in the day so deeply,
is gone.

FINIS.

Endpiece

You can't *really* get to the
Morning Star
On a rocket...

...unless you are Clara.

You can maybe find other ways, though.

They will all be clever ideas.

Acknowledgements

The author would like to express his gratitude to all those who supported this endeavour.

In particular, many thanks to the following people whose help was invaluable in bringing this work to life.

Jean Scott Thomson, Fuchsia Lauren Wilkins,
Peter Alfred Joseph Wilkins, Ashley John West, David Ager,
Andy Fink, David Turner, Atim & Julietta Arden,
Roy Petley, Alex Jakob-Whitworth, Evelyn Clawson,
'Apu' and 'Durga'